For my mum
- K.C.

For Timothy. Wherever you are I am home.
- S.J.

The illustrations in this book were made with watercolors and digital media.
Cataloging-in-Publication Data has been applied
for and may be obtained from the Library of Congress.
ISBN: 978-1-4197-2374-2

ABRAMS The Art of Books
115 West 18th Street, New York, NY 10011
abramsbooks.com

THE
ROAD
HOME

Written by
Katie Cotton

Illustrated by
Sarah Jacoby

ABRAMS BOOKS FOR YOUNG READERS
NEW YORK

Fly **with me** to far away,
where sun still warms the ground.
For winter's in the dying light
and in that windswept sound.

Our wings are sore.
There's far to go
before our flight is flown.

This road is hard, this road is long,
this road that leads us home.

*B*uild **with me** with sticks of straw
and leaves from nearby lands.

Curl them high above our heads —
forget your aching hands.

For safety is a precious place,
a place to call our own.
This road is hard, this road is long,
this road that leads us home.

Hunt with me through light and shade
and hear the woodland cry.
We've claws to grip and jaws to bite,
and prey is close nearby.

For hunger is a burning thing
that settles like a stone.

This road is hard, this road is long,
this road that leads us home.

Come with me through tangled trees
and thorns that grasp our coats.

The air is cold and sharp as ice.
It chills our trembling throats.

For Wolf is near.
His name is Fear.
He wants us for his own.

This road is hard, this road is long,
this road that leads us . . .

. . . home.

Now, at last, we're safe and sound,
tucked in cozy deep.
Let's curl up close, lost in leaves,
lost in velvet sleep.

Another morn, another day,
time to take our flight.
Off we run in sun and sky
and sparkling, dancing light.

This road is hard, this road is long,
but we are not alone.
For you are here, and I'm with you . . .

. . . and so this road is home